HOT DOG and BOB

and the Seriously Scary Attack of the Evil Alien Pizza Person

BY **L. Bob Rovetch** ILLUSTRATED BY **Dave Whamond**

chronicle books · san francisco

Series and book design by Kristine Brogno.
Typeset in Clarendon and Agenda.
The illustrations in this book were rendered in ink,
watercolor washes, and prismacolor.
Manufactured in USA.

Library of Congress Cataloging-in-Publication Data
Rovetch, Lissa.
Hot Dog and Bob and the seriously scary attack of the evil alien pizza
person : adventure #1 / by L. Bob Rovetch ; illustrated by Dave Whamond.
p. cm.
ISBN-13: 978-0-8118-4463-5 (lib. ed.)
ISBN-10: 0-8118-4463-3 (lib. ed.)
ISBN-13: 978-0-8118-5156-5 (pbk.)
ISBN-10: 0-8118-5156-7 (pbk.)
I. Whamond, Dave, ill. II. Title.
2005004041

Distributed in Canada by Raincoast Books
9050 Shaughnessy Street, Vancouver, British Columbia V6P 6E5

10 9 8 7 6 5 4 3 2

Chronicle Books LLC
85 Second Street, San Francisco, California 94105

www.chroniclekids.com

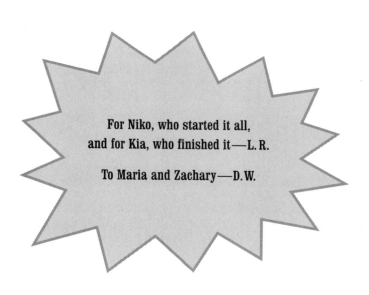

For Niko, who started it all,
and for Kia, who finished it—L. R.

To Maria and Zachary—D. W.

Contents

Chapter 1

Hearing Voices

The day I met Hot Dog was just like every other day at Lugenheimer Elementary School. Right up until lunchtime, that is.

"Yum! A cookie, salami, french fry and banana sandwich with chocolate syrup, ketchup and mayo," said my best friend, Clementine.

"You make the grossest sandwiches," I said.

"They're not gross," said Clementine. "They're creative. Maybe you should try being a little more creative with *your* lunch sometime, Bob."

"No, thanks," I said. "I'm happy with my—"

"Yeah, yeah, don't tell me," said Clementine. "Your peanuts and pizza. You've had the exact same lunch every single day since first grade. I just don't get why you won't ever try anything new."

"Some people like new stuff, and some people like the same stuff," I explained. "I'm a same-stuff kind of a guy. Besides, peanuts are cool. And pizza? Well, just one slice of pepperoni pizza contains—"

"I know, I know," Clementine interrupted me again. "Exactly blah-blah vitamins and blah-blah minerals and blah-di-boring-blah, blah, blah!"

Our friend Marco laughed so hard that milk came squirting out of his nose.

On top of being a same-stuff kind of a guy, I guess you could say I'm also a useless-facts kind of a guy. I remember all kinds of useless stuff, like how many teeth great white sharks have (about 3,000). And how much of the Earth is covered by deserts (about one-fifth). My parents say I have a memory like an elephant. I say that's why I always need to keep plenty of peanuts handy.

Right about then, somewhere between Marco's nose squirting milk and me totally losing my appetite, I heard it.

"Hey, buddy!" a strange voice called. "Would ya hurry up and open this thing? I could use a little air in here."

"What did you say?" I asked Clementine.

"I didn't say anything," Clementine replied.

"Was that you?" I asked Marco.

"Was what me?" Marco asked, wiping milk off his shirt.

"That voice," I said. "Where did that weird-sounding voice come from?"

"In here!" the voice shouted. "Open up your stinkin' lunch box!"

"Whoa! That was a good one," I said to Marco. "How'd you learn to talk without moving your mouth like that?"

"Dude, I told you I didn't say anything," said Marco.

I knew no one could actually be talking to me from inside my lunch box, but I opened it anyway. And that's when my life changed forever. Someone actually *was* talking to me from inside my lunch box. And that someone was a hot dog!

Chapter 2

Partners till the Very End

"What took you so long?" asked the talking hot dog. "A couple more minutes and I woulda been lunch meat!"

I didn't know what to do. I mean, it's not like there's a rule book that tells you how to act if you find a talking hot dog in your lunch box. So I slammed the lid down as fast as I could and pretended nothing was wrong.

"Dude! What's your problem?" asked Marco.

"Are you okay, Bob?" asked Clementine. "You look like you're gonna puke!"

15

"I, um, gotta go," I said, grabbing my lunch box and running out of the lunchroom.

"Have a nice trip!" Barfalot said as I ran by. He stretched out his leg and tripped me with his foot, launching me straight into the trash can. "See ya next fall!"

"'See ya next fall!' That was a good one!" Pigburt and Slugburt giggled.

As you can probably guess, Barfalot, Pigburt and Slugburt—the Terrible Triplets— are dirty, rotten bullies. Barfalot's the leader, and the other two are his brainless body-guards.

THE TERRIBLE TRIPLETS

Slugburt   Barfalot   Pigburt

17

Anyway, I didn't have time to get into a
fight. I climbed out of the trash can, picked up
my lunch box and ran to the boys' bathroom
as fast as I could.

I double-checked to make sure I was alone.
Then I slipped into a stall and locked the door.

I was hoping I'd open my lunch box and realize that the whole thing had just been some kind of weird daydream. But when I looked inside, the hot dog was still there.

"Who are you?" I whispered. "How come you're in my lunch box?"

The strange little guy stood up on my pizza. "Hot Dog's my name, fightin' bad stuff's my game!" he said, with his tiny little hot-dog hands on his tiny little hot-dog hips.

"Ohhh-kaaay," I said.

"Whenever there's big alien trouble on another planet, the Big Bun sends one of us superhero hot dogs from Dogzalot to help out," he said proudly.

"The Big Bun?" I laughed.

"Hey, buster!" the little guy said, shaking his finger at me. "If the Big Bun says you got big trouble, then believe you me, you got big trouble!"

"All right, I believe you! I believe you!" I said. "But how come you're in *my* lunch box?"

"Well, kid, it's like this," he said, sitting down on my bag of peanuts. "I kinda got this, well, this . . . what is it they call it again? Oh, yeah! This little, uh, memory problem."

"Memory problem?" I repeated.

Hot Dog sighed. "Seems on my last mission
I kind of bumped my head on Rocky the Rock
Monster's fists. Hey, how was I supposed to
know the guy's hands were made out of granite?"

Hot Dog sighed again.

"Anyway, the Big Bun says from now on I need backup," Hot Dog explained. "She doesn't trust me to handle the job alone. Says I gotta have a partner with a good memory. You know, just until mine gets back to normal."

"Um, excuse me, Mr. Hot Dog, sir," I said. "Are you saying this, uh, Big Bun picked me to be your partner just because I have a good memory?"

That was pretty hard for me to believe. You'd think if an alien ruler was going to pick a human to save the planet, she'd pick some extra special kid, like my buddy Marco. Marco won the spelling bee for our entire county. Plus, he's the best skateboarder at Lugenheimer Elementary.

But me? Well, I'm just Bob—pretty much your normal, average guy. Bob, who does fine in school, but doesn't take home any awards. Who plays sports, but doesn't score the winning point. Who tries to be nice and stuff, but doesn't *save the world or anything!* And now a super hero hot dog was saying I got picked to be his partner because I have a good memory? Talk about weird!

But unless I was dreaming, weird or not, it was true!

"Listen, kid," Hot Dog said, leaning in close. "You don't have to call me mister. Call me Hot Dog. After all from now on, it's me and you stickin' like glue. Partners till the very end!"

"The very end of w-what?" I asked rather nervously.

"The very end of my mission on your planet, of course," said Hot Dog.

"Oh! *That* very end!" I said. "So, er—what exactly *is* your mission on my planet?"

Just then, the bell rang.

BR-R-RING

I was dying to find out what Hot Dog's mission was, but I'd have to wait. My teacher, Miss Lamphead, hated it when we were late. "Come on," I said. "I gotta get to class. I can't wait to show you to my friends."

"No sirree, Bob!" Hot Dog said, hiding under my pizza. "This mission is top secret. I'll hide out here until the time is right."

"Right," I said, making sure to leave my lunch box open a crack for air.

I took a deep breath and walked down the hall, trying my best to look like someone who didn't have a talking hot dog in his lunch box.

Chapter 3

The Big Cheese

I made it to class just as the late bell rang.

"Is everything all right, Bob?" Miss Lamphead asked nicely.

"Yes, Miss Lamphead," I said, sliding my lunch box under my desk.

"Are you sure, dear?" she asked. "You don't look very well."

"Maybe it was that little trip Bob took to the trash can!" Barfalot yelled out.

"Ha, ha, that's a good one!" Pigburt and Slugburt snorted. "'Little trip to the trash can!' Ha, ha!"

"Please wait your turn to talk, boys," Miss Lamphead said. "I'll call on you just as soon as I can."

Miss Lamphead was always nice and thoughtful, even to the Terrible Triplets. But all of a sudden *she* was the one who didn't look very well.

"Oh, dear," Miss Lamphead said, patting her forehead with her lacy purple handkerchief. "I hope I didn't accidentally eat something with cheese at lunchtime. I'm terribly allergic to cheese, you know."

At first Miss Lamphead just looked kind of pale. But then she started getting sort of yellow and strange looking. Suddenly she stared straight at me with this freaky, wild-eyed expression. Then when she opened her mouth to talk, somebody else's voice came out.

"We do not tolerate late children on Pizzalopolis," she roared. "And we will not tolerate late children here! You will write 'I am extremely dumb

for being late' 437 times in a row. And when you are done with that, you will erase every speck on this floor with your pencil eraser!"

I started feeling sick to my stomach.

"Wow," I heard Hot Dog say. "She's even stricter than the Big Bun!"

"I don't know what's going on," I whispered. "Miss Lamphead's usually really, really nice."

"Excuse me, Miss Lamphead," Clementine said, raising her hand. "What do you mean Pizzalopolis? I thought you were from Nebraska."

"Who said you could talk? You noisy, nosy child!" snapped Miss Lamphead. "*You* will write 'I am extremely dumb for asking questions in school' 964 and a half times. And then you will make lots and lots of tiny little pencil marks on the floor for Late Bob over there to erase."

"Bob and Clementine sittin' in a tree," sang Barfalot, "E-R-A-S-I-N-G!"

"Ha, ha!" snorted Pigburt and Slugburt, who had no clue what E-R-A-S-I-N-G even spelled.

FIG. 1 ----------------------→ FIG. 2 -----------

Well, that's when things got *really* interesting.
Miss Lamphead turned from sort-of yellow to
all-the-way yellow, kind of like cheese. In fact,
exactly like cheese. My teacher was turning
into a gigantic cheese pizza right in front of
our eyes! Pepperoni and all kinds of other

FIG. 3 -▶ FIG. 4...GROSS!

pizza toppings popped up all over her body,
which was getting bigger and rounder every
second. Oh, and did I mention the mozzarella?
Melty mozzarella oozed out of her nostrils.
That was the sickest part of all!

Introducing Cheese Face

I know this whole thing sounds impossible, but it's true. My sweet old teacher had turned into an evil mutant alien pizza person faster than you could say "hold the anchovies." It was like watching a seriously scary horror movie, only there was pizza instead of popcorn, and the movie was real!

Cheese Face (formerly known as Miss Lamphead) planted her big, round body right in front of the classroom door. There was no escape.

POOF!

Chapter 4

Mutant Students

Cheese Face pointed her long, cheesy finger and—ZAP!—the entire row of kids next to the door turned into walking, talking (and, I hate to admit it, but kind of delicious-looking) kid-size pizza slices with hands and feet and faces. The rest of the class totally freaked out. Everyone started screaming.

The icky mutant pizza monster laughed.

"Just a few million more pizza-slice soldiers to follow my every command and I will rule the world!"

I leaned down and whispered into my lunch box. "Um, Hot Dog, I think I might have just figured out what your mission is."

"Like I said," Hot Dog whispered back. "If the Big Bun says you got big trouble, then believe you me, you got big trouble!"

Cheese Face pointed at the desks by the hamster cage, and a bunch more kids turned into pizza soldiers.

Just then I heard a *squeak-squeak* sound coming from the pet corner. I looked over and realized that no one, not even a hamster, was safe from this evil alien's pizza magic. Our

class pet, Esmeralda, was now
a bite-size slice of pizza with
whiskers and a tail.

The pizza-slice kids were walking around
like cheesy zombies. Everyone else raced to
the back of our classroom, away from Cheese
Face. Everyone except Barfalot.

"Hey! No fair!" whined Barfalot, who was
still his regular annoying self. "How come
they get to be pizza soldiers and *I* don't? *I'd*
be better at taking over the world than those
stupid jerks *any* day!"

Cheese Face slowly turned her weird, drippy body to face Barfalot. "You are the whiniest, brattiest, rudest little creature I've met on this worthless planet so far," she said in a low, creepy voice. Then she smiled. "I like it! I'm going to make you the general of my army. *I* will boss *you* around, and *you* will boss *them* around."

And with one point of Cheese Face's famous finger, my least favorite person in this entire world became my very worst nightmare: *General* Barfalot, uniform, tomato sauce and all.

Chapter 4½

It's All in the Timing

"Oh, goody gumdrops," said Clementine. "Not only do I get to become an unattractive food item, I also get to be bossed around by a dork with the IQ of a freckle's freckle."

Clementine was right. Seeing sweet old Miss Lamphead transformed into a mutant pizza was bad. Watching my friends turn into pizza-slice zombies was even worse. But having to follow Barfalot's orders, now *that* was going too far.

"I don't want to tell you how to do your job or anything," I whispered into my lunch box.

"But isn't this the part where you're supposed to come in?"

"It's all in the timing," said Hot Dog. "Just watch and learn, kid. Just watch and learn."

"Hey, you! Late Boy!" Cheese Face belched. "Wanna tell the rest of the class why you're talking to a lunch box?"

"N-n-n-no th-thank you," I stuttered.

"OPEN IT!" she shouted.

Now I know I'd only known Hot Dog since lunchtime, but a guy has to protect his

partner, right? I mean I couldn't let down the Big Bun, could I?

"No!" I said. "I won't!"

"Then I'll open it myself!" Cheese Face said, snatching the lunch box out of my hands.

And that's when things got really, *really* interesting.

Chapter 5

Flying Weenie to the Rescue

My lunch box exploded open, and Hot Dog flew into the air. "This pizza party's over!" he announced, just like a real superhero.

"Who's the flying weenie?" asked Marco.

"That's no flying weenie," I said. "That's my partner, Hot Dog. He's going to save us!"

"Ohhh-kaaay," said Clementine. "But if *he's* our only chance, I'm not exactly getting my hopes up."

Cheese Face tried to zap Hot Dog. But Hot Dog kept flying around the classroom, doing triple flips and fancy loops. Cheese Face missed every time.

"Whoa! Awesome tricks!" said Marco.
"Somebody get that little dude a skateboard!"

"Okay, back me up here, partner," Hot Dog
called down to me.

"What do I do?" I called back.

"You're the one with the memory," said Hot
Dog. "Just remember the plan!"

"What plan?" I panicked. "You never told me
the plan!"

"Are you sure?" said Hot Dog. "I could have
sworn I told you the plan."

"Believe me," I said. "You never told me the plan!"

"Oops! My mistake!" Hot Dog said, zipping around Cheese Face's drippy, grabbing hands. "Now let's see—what was the plan again?"

Clementine rolled her eyes and gave me this look. It was a this-flying-weenie-is-off-his-rocker-and-we're-doomed-for-sure kind of a look.

I wished that when the Big Bun was up there on Dogzalot choosing a superhero hot dog to save our planet, she had picked one who still had a memory and didn't *need* a partner. But no such luck.

Just then Hot Dog said, "I remember now! The plan is Combo Number Five!"

"GOTCHA!" Cheese Face cried. She had Hot Dog trapped in one hand. The other hand was busy zapping the remaining kids into pizza-slice soldiers.

Finally she turned to Clementine, Marco and me.

"Twenty-four down and three to go!" She laughed and pointed straight at us. Hot Dog struggled to free himself from her grip, but it was no use.

I held my breath, closed my eyes and waited. When I opened my eyes, Marco was pizza. But for some reason, Clementine and I were still people! Luckily, Cheese Face was too busy celebrating her victory with her zombie pizza army to notice that Clementine and I hadn't been zapped into pizza soldiers, too. We crawled behind a bookcase to hide.

"How come we're not pizza?" whispered Clementine.

"I don't know," I whispered back. "Maybe being Hot Dog's partner and Hot Dog's partner's friend makes us immune to Cheese Face's zapping or something."

"I just hope we live long enough to find out the answer," said Clementine.

"Today Miss Lamphead's class, tomorrow the world!" Cheese Face belched, holding Hot Dog high in the air like a trophy.

"Today Miss Lamphead's class, tomorrow the world!" repeated the pizza-slice army.

"I don't think so!" Hot Dog said. He'd managed to free one arm, reach inside his bun and push a hidden button. A gigantic glob of spicy mustard squirted right up Cheese Face's nose.

"RRRRRAAAAAAAHHHHHHHHH!" Cheese Face screamed, flinging Hot Dog through the air.

I watched helplessly as my poor little partner sailed across the room. He slammed into the blackboard with a splat.

"NO-OOOO!!!" I wailed. "YOU KILLED MY PARTNER!!!"

55

Chapter 6

Mozzarella Misery

I ran straight for poor, dead Hot Dog.

"Bob! Stop!" Clementine hissed from our hiding place. "What are you doing?"

To be honest, I didn't even think about what I was doing until it was way too late. Just before I reached my dearly departed partner, Cheese Face dropped a sick blob of mozzarella right on top of me. I was completely stuck in a disgusting, cheesy prison, and there was no more superhero left to save me—or the rest of the planet.

It was official. Cheese Face was taking over the world, and it was *not* going to be pretty!

"Victory to the pizza people!" Cheese Face
cheered.

"Victory to the pizza people!" her army
repeated.

Now there was only one hope left. Clementine
bravely crawled toward me under the desks.
When she reached my sticky prison, she used

the only weapon against cheese she could find
. . . her teeth.

As Clementine chomped and chewed away at
my cheesy prison, I stood there with one stupid
thought in my head: "I want my mommy!!!"
Clementine was doing her best, but no way
could anybody eat through THAT much
cheese—not even Clementine.

As the seconds passed, mozzarella dripped down my face. I was running out of air. I was running out of time! I had to face facts. I wasn't going to see my mom, my dad, my good old dog Chomper or my annoying little brother Bug ever again.

I was just about to give up when I saw the most beautiful sight I'd ever seen: Clementine's pearly white teeth. She actually did it. I was free!

Now I wouldn't blame you for having a hard time believing that a regular kid with regular teeth and a regular stomach could eat through enough cheese in a couple of minutes to free another kid who's covered in the stuff. But that's Clementine for you. I don't know, maybe all her years of eating those gross "creative" lunches prepared her for that moment. But I do know this: That girl can eat!

As soon as I was free, I ran to Hot Dog. "You gave it your best shot, partner," I whispered, scooping his limp little body off the floor. "And I'm going to make sure you get a real superhero's funeral, because even though you didn't actually save our class or our planet, you died trying."

"Shhh," Clementine said. She signaled me to follow her under the desks. I carefully put Hot Dog in my pocket and started crawling. We were almost at the door, just a few inches from freedom, when—

"Stop right there!" General Barfalot said. "You two don't go anywhere unless *I* say so!"

"Get them!" Cheese Face commanded.

63

Chapter 7

He's Alive!

Barfalot and all the other pizza soldiers started marching toward us. We were cornered. But I had an idea.

I reached into my pocket and pulled out a bunch of peanuts.

"Peanuts!" I said to Clementine. "I told you peanuts were cool!"

"Trust me," Clementine hissed. "This *really* isn't the time to be talking about peanuts!"

"Don't be so sure," I said, tossing a handful of nuts on the floor.

The soldiers started slipping and sliding all over the place. I threw out another handful.

KA-BLAM! General Barfalot and his entire army fell down like a bunch of bowling pins.

"Yes!" said Clementine. "Let's make a break for it!"

We opened the door and ran. But we didn't get far. Cheese Face's stretchy arm reached clear down the hallway and wrapped around us like a boa constrictor. She pulled us back into the classroom, smiling her sickening, gooey smile. "Too bad your silly little super-

hero is deader than a doorknob. Nobody can help you or your pitiful little planet now."

"Oh, I wouldn't be so sure about that," Hot Dog said, zooming out of my pocket.

"Cool! The flying weenie's okay!" said Clementine.

"Hot Dog!" I said. "You're alive!"

"General Barfalot!" yelled Cheese Face. "I order you to get rid of that annoying little pest once and for all!"

Barfalot saluted. "Immediately, Your Cheesiness!" He nodded at Pigburt and Slugburt.

The three mozzarella meanies started chasing Hot Dog around the room, clapping their hands together like they were trying to swat a mosquito. Only instead of smashing Hot Dog, they just kept smashing each other. It was totally awesome!

"You know, all this exercise is making me kinda hungry," Hot Dog said. "Anyone care for a little snack?"

He reached inside his bun and pushed
another button. In seconds, Barfalot and his
brainless bodyguards were buried up to their
necks in relish. Then Hot Dog turned his bun
bottons toward Cheese Face.

Cheese Face just laughed. "Do what you want with those useless little soldiers. Soon I shall have scrillions more just like them!"

"In your dreams!" Hot Dog replied. He pushed even more bun buttons, and every hot-dog topping imaginable came shooting out. Clementine and I climbed up on top of the art-supply cabinet so we wouldn't drown in the rising river of ketchup, sauerkraut, onions, mustard, mayonnaise and relish.

The pizza-slice kids were light enough to stay afloat in the sick sea of slime. But Cheese Face didn't float. Her huge body sank down, down, down into the gross gook. We waited and watched for a long, long time, but she stayed sunk.

At last, the nightmare was over.

Chapter 8

She's Alive!

"Well, partner," said Hot Dog. "It looks like we didn't need the plan after all."

"Wait a minute," I said. "What's making those bubbles?" I pointed at the spot of goo where Cheese Face had disappeared. Was that the top of Cheese Face's head?

"Oh, no!" cried Clementine. "She's back!"

"Quick! The plan!" I screamed at Hot Dog.

Hot Dog was hanging on to Miss Lamp-head's favorite rain-forest mobile, mumbling, "Plan, plan, think, think, must remember plan."

"Combo Number Five!" I shouted. "The plan is Combo Number Five!"

I had no idea what "Combo Number Five" meant. I knew thousands of random facts, but not this one. Was it the first letter of a combination lock that held the key to destroying Cheese Face? Or some kind of signal for the Big Bun to send a *real* superhero to come save us? All I could do was cross my fingers and hope that Hot Dog remembered what it meant. Did he???

BACK IN A
FLASH!

"Thanks, partner!" Hot Dog said. "I'll be back in a flash!" He waved good-bye and flew out the window.

"Back in a flash? Back in a flash? He can't be serious!" Clementine howled. "*We're* going to be *pizza* in a flash! Wonderful superhero you got yourself there, Bob. The world's about to end, and he decides to take a little break!"

just stayed in bed," I kept thinking. "If only, if only..."

Just then, Hot Dog crashed back in through the window, joining us in the stinky cave of Cheese Face's mouth just before it closed shut.

"Sorry it took me so long," he said, catching his breath. "But you should have seen the line at Mr. Chang's Yummy Garden Restaurant. It took *forever* to get this chow mein, wonton soup, egg roll and fortune cookie."

"I don't believe it!" yelled Clementine. "The world's about to end, and *you're* stopping for takeout?"

"This isn't just any takeout," said Hot Dog. "This is Combo Number Five!"

"Do you actually expect us to believe that chow mein is going to save the world?" asked Clementine.

"Yep!" Hot Dog smiled. Then he jumped straight down Cheese Face's throat, Combo Number Five and all.

Chapter 9

Barf-o-Rama

Seconds after Hot Dog took the plunge, Cheese Face made a spooky, whale-dying-in-a-thunderstorm kind of a noise. The stinky cave opened right up and Clementine and I jumped out of Cheese Face's mouth.

"I don't know if that was really, really brave or really, really stupid of Hot Dog," I said.

Cheese Face's belly started rumbling. The whole room rocked, rattled and rolled. It felt like we were in a radical earthquake. Then— "BLEEEGGGHHH!!!" It was the biggest grand-daddy burp of all time.

Hot Dog shot out of Cheese Face's mouth like a cannonball. Then everyone Cheese Face had gobbled up oozed right back out of her mouth in a sticky stream of goo. But they weren't coming out as pizza soldiers. They were coming out as their regular human selves!

"I know this isn't exactly the best time for bad jokes," said Clementine. "But don't you think it's funny that Barfalot just got barfed—a lot?"

Cheese Face didn't stop hurling. She kept right on going until there was nothing left of her at all. In the end, all that remained was poor old Miss Lamphead standing in a puddle of yuckiness, looking seriously confused.

"What just happened?" Clementine asked Hot Dog.

"It's simple," Hot Dog answered. "Everyone knows that the only way to stop an evil mutant alien from Pizzalopolis is with a precise mixture of ingredients: chow mein, wonton soup, egg roll and fortune cookie, otherwise known as—"

"Combo Number Five!" Clementine and I jinxed each other.

"But I couldn't have done it without your memory, partner!" Hot Dog said. "Or your quick thinking, Clementine."

"Thanks." Clementine smiled proudly.

"Well, I guess it's cleanup time," said Hot Dog. He pushed yet another bun button, and the coolest rain-but-not-rain shower poured down on everyone and everything except Clementine and me. The river of goo was gone, Cheese Face was gone and, last but not least, Hot Dog was gone.

Miss Lamphead cleared her throat, blew her nose into her lacy purple handkerchief and said, "Now, where was I again, class? Oh, yes, I believe I was collecting your math homework. My goodness, it's so warm in this room. Let's open a few windows and let some air in, shall we?"

Spicy Hamster

Other than the fact that kids kept finding mysterious bits of pepperoni and olives in their hair, Hot Dog's cleanup shower seemed to make everybody forget all about the disgusting Cheese Face disaster. Everything went back to normal at Lugenheimer Elementary School. Except, that is, for our class pet, Esmeralda. She smelled so spicy and delicious nobody could hold her without licking her. Miss Lamphead got so tired of sending students to the nurse's office with hamster bites on their tongues that she declared Esmeralda off-limits and got the class a goldfish for the pet corner instead.

Chapter 10
One More Time

A couple of months later Clementine threw her string cheese at me in the cafeteria.

"Want this?" she asked. "I've told my mom a thousand times I don't eat this stuff anymore, but she keeps sticking it in my lunch anyway."

"I know what you mean," I said. "My mom still asks what made me switch from pizza to Chinese food."

"Why don't you just tell her the truth?" asked Clementine. "Pizza makes you sick now because it reminds you of Cheese Face. And Chinese food is cool because a flying weenie used it to save your life."

"Yeah, she'll definitely believe that!" I laughed. I was glad I wasn't the only one who had escaped Hot Dog's forgetting shower. Without Clementine to back me up, I'd probably think I had imagined the whole thing. "You know, I still wonder why we were the only ones who weren't affected by any of that weird stuff."

"I know," said Clementine. "Sometimes I even wish I could see Hot Dog one more time, just to ask him."

"Will you two quit your yappin' and open this thing up?" said a voice.

I looked at Clementine. "It can't be," I said.

"Why not?" she said. "It's happened before."

I cracked my lunch box open an inch and whispered into it, "Please, *please* tell me you just popped by to say hello."

"Sorry, partner, there's no time for small talk," said Hot Dog. "The Big Bun says you got big trouble, and—"

"I know, don't tell me," I groaned.
"If the Big Bun says you got big
trouble, then believe you me, you got
big trouble!"

THE
END

(Or should I say, The Beginning?)

To be continued . . .

L. Bob Rovetch and her brilliant advisers, Kia and Niko, live across the Golden Gate Bridge from San Francisco. When she isn't busy looking after her crazy puppies, man-eating lovebird, and mystery pet, L. Bob enjoys having burping contests with her family.

Dave Whamond wanted to be a cartoonist ever since he could pick up a crayon. During math classes he would doodle in the margins of his papers. One math teacher warned him, "You'd better spend more time on your math and less time cartooning. You can't make a living drawing funny pictures." Today Dave has a syndicated daily comic strip called "Reality Check."

Dave has one wife, two kids, one dog, and one kidney. They all live together in Calgary, Alberta.